ESSENTIAL
MAMMALS

by Marie Pearson

CONTENT CONSULTANT
Dr. Hayley C. Lanier
Assistant Professor of Biology
Assistant Curator of Mammalogy, Sam Noble Museum
Department of Biology
The University of Oklahoma

ESSENTIAL ANIMALS

Essential Library

An Imprint of Abdo Publishing
abdobooks.com

abdobooks.com

Published by Abdo Publishing, a division of ABDO, PO Box 398166, Minneapolis, Minnesota 55439. Copyright © 2022 by Abdo Consulting Group, Inc. International copyrights reserved in all countries. No part of this book may be reproduced in any form without written permission from the publisher. Essential Library™ is a trademark and logo of Abdo Publishing.

Printed in the United States of America, North Mankato, Minnesota.
102021
012022

THIS BOOK CONTAINS RECYCLED MATERIALS

Cover Photos: Shutterstock Images (elephant), (dolphin); Igor Cheri/Shutterstock Images (bat); Eric Isselee/Shutterstock Images (lemur), (dog); Stepan Kapl/Shutterstock Images (tiger)
Interior Photos: Eric Isselee/Shutterstock Images, 1, 20, 69; Wild Media/Shutterstock Images, 4; Craig Lambert Photography/Shutterstock Images, 5; Dede Sudiana/Shutterstock Images, 8; Shutterstock Images, 10, 30, 34, 38, 40, 42, 44, 46 (standard poodle), 47, 49, 64, 67, 72, 103 (rabbit); Rich Carey/Shutterstock Images, 11; Karel Bartik/Shutterstock Images, 12; Michael Potter/Shutterstock Images, 14, 103 (elephant); Dmitry Pichugin/Shutterstock Images, 15; Frank Fichtmueller/Shutterstock Images, 16, 102 (beaver); Viktor Loki/Shutterstock Images, 17; Karen Crewe/iStockphoto, 18; NHPA/Photoshot/Science Source, 21, 91, 103 (rat); Tim Vernon/Science Source, 22; blickwinkel/Hecker/Alamy, 23; SCIEPRO/Science Source, 24, 26, 102 (whale); Chase Dekker/Shutterstock Images, 27; Tory Kallman/Shutterstock Images, 28, 102 (dolphin); Vladimir Wrangel/Shutterstock Images, 31; Lukas Kovarik/Shutterstock Images, 32, 102 (sloth); Frank McClintock/Shutterstock Images, 33; Bruno Vieira/Shutterstock Images, 36, 102 (capybara); Jurgens Potgieter/Shutterstock Images, 37; Astrid Gast/Shutterstock Images, 41, 103 (cat); Lesia Kapinosova/Shutterstock Images, 46 (Chihuahua), 102 (Chihuahua); Ricant Images/Shutterstock Images, 46 (mastiff); Belu Gheorghe/Shutterstock Images, 46 (Great Dane); iStockphoto, 46 (dachshund), 55, 65, 77, 78, 96, 99, 103 (rhinoceros), 103 (tiger); Sofia Dudova/Shutterstock Images, 46 (Samoyed); Peter Adams Photography/Shutterstock Images, 48, 103 (dromedary); Lal Nallath/Shutterstock Images, 50; Martin Pelanek/Shutterstock Images, 52; Tom McHugh/Science Source, 54, 103 (platypus); Mary Ann McDonald/Shutterstock Images, 56; Red Line Editorial, 57, 93, 102–103; Jurgen Vogt/Shutterstock Images, 58, 103 (gorilla); Sam Chow/Shutterstock Images, 60; Paul Staniszewski/Shutterstock Images, 61, 102 (elk); Ronnie Howard/Shutterstock Images, 62; Weekend Warrior Photos/Shutterstock Images, 63; Anthony Mercieca/Science Source, 68; Dr. Thomas Spaeter/Shutterstock Images, 70, 103 (hedgehog); Csanad Kiss/Shutterstock Images, 71; Erica Hollingshead/Shutterstock Images, 73, 103 (horse); Grobler du Preez/Shutterstock Images, 74–75; Kay Durden/iStockphoto, 76; William J. Weber/iStockphoto, 80; Liz Weber/Shutterstock Images, 81, 102 (bat); Ted Kinsman/Science Source, 82; MerlinTuttle.org/Science Source, 83; Leonardo Mercon/Shutterstock Images, 84; John Serrao/Science Source, 85, 102 (armadillo); Ivan Kuzmin/Science Source, 86; Benny Marty/Shutterstock Images, 88, 103 (kangaroo); John Carnemolla/Shutterstock Images, 89; No Limit Pictures/iStockphoto, 92, 103 (lemur); Mikhail Blajenov/Shutterstock Images, 94; Gudkov Andrey/Shutterstock Images, 98

Editor: Arnold Ringstad
Series Designer: Sarah Taplin

Library of Congress Control Number: 2020949101

Publisher's Cataloging-in-Publication Data

Names: Pearson, Marie, author.
Title: Essential mammals / by Marie Pearson
Description: Minneapolis, Minnesota : Abdo Publishing, 2022 | Series: Essential animals | Includes online resources and index.
Identifiers: ISBN 9781532195549 (lib. bdg.) | ISBN 9781098215927 (ebook)
Subjects: LCSH: Mammals--Juvenile literature. | Mammals--Behavior--Juvenile literature. | Animals--Identification--Juvenile literature. | Zoology--Juvenile literature.
Classification: DDC 599--dc23

CONTENTS

INTRODUCTION 4

AFRICAN BUSH ELEPHANT 12

AMERICAN BEAVER 16

BLACK RAT 20

BLUE WHALE 24

BOTTLENOSE DOLPHIN 28

BROWN-THROATED THREE-TOED SLOTH 32

CAPYBARA 36

CAT 40

DOG 44

DROMEDARY 48

DUCK-BILLED PLATYPUS 52

EASTERN GORILLA 56

ELK 60

EUROPEAN RABBIT 64

FOUR-TOED HEDGEHOG 68

HORSE 72

INDIAN RHINOCEROS 76

LITTLE BROWN BAT 80

NINE-BANDED ARMADILLO 84

RED KANGAROO 88

RING-TAILED LEMUR 92

TIGER 96

ESSENTIAL FACTS 100
MAMMALS AROUND THE WORLD 102
GLOSSARY 104
ADDITIONAL RESOURCES 106

SOURCE NOTES 108
INDEX 110
ABOUT THE AUTHOR 112
ABOUT THE CONSULTANT 112

INTRODUCTION

Many mammal species, including brown bears, care for their young as the young mature.

From the Arctic Ocean to the treetops of the Amazon rain forest and the hot sands of the Sahara desert, mammals make their homes in every major habitat on Earth. Some mammals swim in rivers or oceans. Some climb mountains, while others fly or glide from tree to tree. Mammals burrow underground and run or jump aboveground. This diverse group of animals has captured the hearts of many people and played important roles in human history. In fact, humans themselves are mammals.

Mammals have long provided humans with food, clothing, transportation, and companionship. The first animals to be domesticated were mammals. Mammals have been a source of various forms of entertainment to humans as well. Humans have hunted certain species for sport. People also enjoy portraying mammals in art.

INTRODUCTION

Depictions of mammals have been found in the oldest known cave paintings. Today, many people simply enjoy spotting mammals in their natural habitats. Tourists flock to parks in Africa hoping to catch a glimpse of the magnificent mammals that live there.

Scientists classify living things based on how closely they are related. The basic categories, from broadest to most specific, are domain, kingdom, phylum, class, order, family, genus, and species. Mammals are all the animals in the class Mammalia. This class is divided into approximately 26 orders, depending on which system is used.[1] In 2020, there were more than 6,300 known living species of mammals.[2] This may seem like a lot. But there are other animal classes with even more known living species. There are

INTRODUCTION

more than 8,200 known amphibian species.[3] And there are more than one million known insect species.[4] Despite their relatively low numbers, mammals play important roles in their habitats.

WHAT MAKES A MAMMAL?

All mammals have three things in common. First, they all have hair at some point in their lives. Hair can also be called fur. Most mammals, such as foxes and bison, have thick coats of hair. Other mammals, such as whales and elephants, may appear hairless. However, a close-up look reveals they do have scattered bristles of hair. Hair grows from the skin and is made from the protein keratin. No other animals have the same type of hair that mammals have.

FUN FACT
Sea otters have up to one million hairs per square inch. The figure for dogs is about 60,000.[5]

A coat of hair can protect a mammal against extreme cold and heat. It can also provide camouflage. In addition to body hair, some mammals have special hairs called whiskers. Whiskers can tell mammals information about the objects they brush against, including size and shape. Some mammals even have hair in the form of spines, such as those on porcupines.

A second shared characteristic in mammals is a set of three middle ear bones. A mammal has a flap of skin and cartilage around a hole going into its head. In the middle ear, a membrane covers the hole. On the other side of the membrane is an air-filled chamber with three middle ear bones. The bones are the malleus, incus, and stapes. These bones transfer sound waves to the inner ear. The inner ear has the nerves that allow animals to hear sounds. Other animals, such as reptiles and birds, have only one bone in the middle ear.

The third shared characteristic is that all female mammals produce milk from mammary glands. They feed their young with this milk. Milk has fats and proteins. Baby mammals need this milk to survive and grow.

There are a few more traits that most, but not all, mammals share. A mammal's lower jaw consists of a single bone known as a dentary. Mammals also typically have good senses of sight, smell, hearing, and touch. They rely on these senses to find food, detect threats, communicate, and select mates.

GROUPS OF MAMMALS

Mammals are divided into three basic groups. These groups are placental mammals, marsupials, and monotremes. Most mammal species are placental mammals. A placental mammal develops in its mother's uterus until the mother gives birth. While a mammal is growing in the uterus, it gets nutrients from the mother through an organ called the placenta. After

MAMMAL EXTREMES

Mammals are an incredibly diverse group of animals. The smallest are certain types of bats and shrews, which may weigh as little as 0.1 ounces (3 g). The largest animal on Earth is a mammal, the blue whale. It weighs 176 tons (160 metric tons).[6] A cheetah is the fastest land animal. It can run up to 70 miles per hour (113 kmh) in short bursts.[7] Meanwhile, a three-toed sloth might only reach 0.17 miles per hour (0.27 kmh).[8] Mammals may get around on two legs, on four legs, or with flippers.

INTRODUCTION

some time, the mother gives birth to live young. Bears, horses, and humans are examples of placental mammals.

Marsupials also develop in the uterus for a time. As with placental mammals, a baby marsupial gets nutrients from a placenta while in the uterus. Marsupials give birth to live young, but when a marsupial is born, it is far less developed than a placental mammal. It must crawl to its mother's teats. It latches on to a nipple. The nipple swells and becomes very difficult to separate from the baby's mouth. The baby stays there for weeks or months.

It nurses and develops through the same final stages that a placental mammal would spend in its mother's uterus. Some marsupials, such as kangaroos, have pouches covering the nipples. Others, such as certain opossum species, do not have pouches. The young must remain firmly attached to the nipple.

Monotremes have the fewest species of the three mammal groups. There are just five living monotreme species.

Nearly all mammal species give birth to live young.

These include the duck-billed platypus and four types of echidnas. Unlike other mammals, monotremes do not give birth to live young. Instead, they lay eggs. Some lay eggs in burrows. Others carry eggs in pouches. After the young hatch, mothers feed them milk.

Regardless of how their offspring are born, all female mammals care for their young. Mothers protect their young and teach them important skills and behaviors. Males in some species help raise young too. In other species, males do not.

BEHAVIORS

Since all mammals are raised by their mothers, they are able to learn things that are not purely instinct. Mothers and other adults can teach young what foods to eat and where to find them. The ability to learn from adults is one reason that mammals have survived in so many environments.

As adults, mammals may live alone or in groups. Those in groups typically have social structures. Some animals are more dominant than others. They must fight or perform certain patterns of behavior to keep dominance within their social structures.

Typically a single male will mate with multiple females. For this reason, only a few males may breed in a season. Females are also often selective in which males they accept as mates. Males often fight with each other for the opportunity to breed. The male who is more powerful usually gets the chance to breed. Because this competition leads to the natural selection of certain traits in males, male mammals often look different from females.

INTRODUCTION

Whether they live in groups or alone, communication is important for mammals. Communication helps mammals establish social dominance. It also helps mammals find mates and keep other mammals away from their territories. Mammals can communicate with one another through body language, vocalizations, and scents.

MAMMALS AND HUMANS

Some mammals are pests. They eat crops or livestock that people raise for food and income. They may cause damage if they cross the road in front of a vehicle. Some destroy property by chewing wires and insulation. Mammals may also spread diseases to livestock and humans. For example, rabies can kill both livestock and humans.

Humans—who are themselves mammals—often keep mammals such as cats and dogs as pets.

Mammals that are seen as pests may be targeted by people. People may hunt predators such as wolves and tigers, which sometimes kill livestock. Uncontrolled hunting has driven some species close to extinction. In addition, as the human population increases, more land is being used for agricultural fields, roads, and buildings. Human activity helps transport diseases between populations of mammals. Some mammal habitats are being split apart or are disappearing altogether. This can make it hard for animals to find food or mates.

ESSENTIAL MAMMALS

This book presents 22 notable mammal species from around the world. The species are presented alphabetically by their common names. These mammals represent the amazing diversity of appearance and behavior in the class Mammalia. These animals range in size from the small black rat to the enormous blue whale. Some, such as the dog, are seen commonly in everyday life. Others, such as the eastern gorilla, live only in remote places. Each species plays an important role in its ecosystem. Narrative stories, colorful photos, fact boxes, and the latest scientific findings help bring to life the hairy animals that have been inspiring people throughout human history.

The destruction of habitats threatens mammals and other types of animals that live in these places.

AFRICAN BUSH ELEPHANT

Elephants can dig to reach water sources if they need to.

A herd of 15 African bush elephants wanders along a dry riverbed in Namibia. The elephants need water. They use their tusks, trunks, and feet to start digging holes in the dry riverbed. They dig until they reach water. This water is cleaner than that in open pools nearby. An elephant sticks its trunk in a hole and sucks up approximately 2.6 gallons (10 L) of water. Then it lifts the end of its trunk to its mouth and squirts the water out.

Once the herd has had enough to drink, the elephants leave the water holes. They use their trunks to suck up dust near the riverbed. They spray the dust over their backs. This protects their skin from the sun's damaging rays and from biting insects. Meanwhile, antelopes and other animals gather at the holes the elephants dug. They drink their fill of fresh water. The elephants help other animals survive in the dry climate.

MASSIVE MAMMALS

African bush elephants are the largest land mammals. They can weigh up to 6.7 tons (6.1 metric tons). That is approximately the weight of four small SUVs. Their huge bodies are covered in gray skin with scattered, bristly hair.

An elephant's nose and upper lip form its trunk. The trunk can be used to grasp objects such as food. It is also used to breathe and can act like a snorkel when the elephant swims. Males and females both grow a pair of modified teeth called tusks. The tusks are made of ivory. In addition to being useful for digging, tusks can help elephants defend themselves from other elephants or from predators such as lions.

African bush elephants cannot sweat. Sweating would cause them to quickly become dehydrated in their arid habitats. But they have another way to cool off. Large, thin flaps of skin form their ears. These ears can fan an elephant's body. Because they are thin, they

FUN FACT

Elephants eat as much as 300 pounds (140 kg) of food every day.[9]

AFRICAN BUSH ELEPHANT

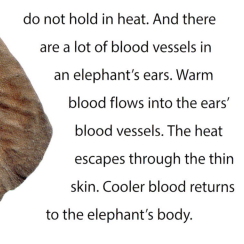

do not hold in heat. And there are a lot of blood vessels in an elephant's ears. Warm blood flows into the ears' blood vessels. The heat escapes through the thin skin. Cooler blood returns to the elephant's body.

ELEPHANT FAMILIES

A female elephant typically has a single baby at a time. Calves already weigh 200 pounds (90 kg) when they are born. They nurse for three years but also eat other food. They become independent of their mothers at eight years old. Females will stay with the herd through adulthood. A herd of females can have as many as 70 individuals.[10] At approximately ten years of age, males leave to live on their own or with a small herd of other males.

African bush elephants sleep four hours a day. The rest of their time is spent eating, drinking, and spraying water, mud, or dust onto their skin. Because they live in groups, communication is important. They use body language and various sounds. A trumpeting sound can be a sign of aggression. Using a specialized pouch in its throat, an elephant can also make sounds at frequencies too low for humans to hear. These sounds can travel up to 2.5 miles (4 km).[11] They help elephants find mates. They also help keep herds together.

Elephants are highly social creatures.

AFRICAN BUSH ELEPHANT
Loxodonta africana

SIZE
Males 10.5–13 feet (3.2–4 m) tall at the shoulder; females 7.2–8.5 feet (2.2–2.6 m)

WEIGHT
Males 5–6.7 tons (4.5–6.1 metric tons); females 2.2–3.9 tons (2–3.5 metric tons)

RANGE
Central and southern Africa

HABITAT
Deserts, savannas, scrub forests, woodlands, rain forests

DIET
Leaves, twigs, roots, bark, grasses, fruits, herbs

LIFE SPAN
70 years on average in the wild; 80 years on average in captivity

AMERICAN BEAVER

Beavers are well known in pop culture for their ability to chew through wood and build dams.

The American beaver searches along the edge of a stream at night. The rodent finds a thin tree. It begins chewing around the tree's base, munching deeper and deeper into the wood until the tree finally falls over. The beaver chews off branches and drags them into the stream. It also pushes up mud. The branches and mud form a dam, blocking water from flowing in its original path. The water pools behind the dam and makes a pond.

Now the beaver can build its lodge in the pond. The water here is calmer than in a stream. This helps keep the lodge intact. The water is also deeper. This keeps potential predators from reaching the lodge. The beaver piles up sticks in the pond. Water surrounds the sticks on all sides. The rodent uses mud to cement the branches together. The mud also helps keep the inside of the lodge dry. The lodge has a central room that can be as wide as 8 feet (2 m).[12] The room is above water level. Bark and wood chips cover the floor. A small hole in the top lets in fresh air. The beaver makes a couple of entrances to its lodge. The entrances are underwater. This keeps predators out. The lodge will keep the beaver warm and safe in the winter.

A large beaver lodge in Alaska

AMERICAN BEAVER

AQUATIC RODENTS

American beavers make their homes in the water. Their bodies are adapted to their habitats. Their dense, brown coats keep them warm. A beaver has a gland near its anus that produces oil. The beaver spreads this oil over its coat to make it waterproof. A beaver can close its small ears when it goes underwater. Each eye has a clear membrane that covers and protects the eye while the beaver swims. The beaver's tail is shaped like a paddle and is covered in scales. The tail helps with swimming. Beavers also use their tails to communicate, slapping them on the water to let each other know if danger is nearby. A beaver's large, webbed back feet help it swim too. Beavers can stay underwater for as long as 15 minutes.[13]

FUN FACT

Beavers are monogamous. This means they keep the same mate year after year until one of them dies.

18

Beavers don't spend time only in the water. They need to get around on land too. Their small front feet have claws for digging. They can grip things with their front feet. A beaver's top front teeth are large and orange. They constantly grow. Chewing on trees keeps the teeth from growing too long.

LIFE AS A BEAVER

Beavers live in family groups of up to eight members. These groups are called colonies. A colony is made up of a male, a female, and their young. The young are known as kits. Typically the young include the kits born in the current year and the kits born in the previous year. Beavers in a colony often help groom one another.

In the winter, beavers spend most of their time in the lodge. Its walls freeze solid, which helps keep the room inside warmer. Beavers are strictly herbivores, and during the winter they mainly eat branches that they have stored underwater.

Beavers are not currently at risk of extinction. But in the past, they were heavily hunted for their fur. Very few were left in the wild by 1900. Since then, people have helped reintroduce beavers into many regions.

AMERICAN BEAVER
Castor canadensis

SIZE
35–46 inches (89–117 cm) from nose to tail

WEIGHT
29–71 pounds (13–32 kg)

RANGE
North America

HABITAT
Lakes, ponds, streams

DIET
Tree bark, tissues growing under the tree bark, water plants, roots, flower buds

LIFE SPAN
10–20 years in the wild

BLACK RAT

Black rats are generally considered pests, but some people keep them as pets.

Night has fallen. Black rats have found a hole in the grain store. The gap is only as wide as a human thumb, but the rats can squeeze through. Mountains of wheat lie inside the building. The rats feast on the grain, and as they eat, they also urinate and defecate on the piles of food.

Early the next morning, before the sun has risen, the grain store manager arrives at the building to check on the grain. The rats hear the manager coming and scurry back into hiding. The manager sees the droppings the rats left behind. He knows he will have to get rid of the rats. They could destroy the grain. Their urine can carry many diseases that can affect humans and other animals. If there are a lot of rats, they may even eat enough grain to reduce the manager's profits when it is sold.

APPEARANCE AND SPREAD

Black rats are smaller than the Norway rat, which is the most common type in urban areas today. Black rats are typically black, but they can also be gray or grayish brown, have white spots, or have a pattern called agouti, which is multiple bands of color on a single hair. The rats' rounded ears and long tails are mostly hairless.

Scientists think these rats are native to India and the surrounding region. Human travel began carrying them around the world long ago. They may have reached what is now the United Kingdom by the 200s CE. Black rats infested ships. As the ships docked at ports, some rats ended up in coastal cities. Black

By climbing aboard ships and traveling to new lands, rats have spread disease.

rats carry the fleas that spread bubonic plague, a deadly disease that has killed millions of people. During the mid-1300s CE in Europe, the plague killed approximately one-third of the European population. Scientists have said the travel of black rats contributed to the plague's spread. Fleas that lived on the rats would sometimes bite humans, giving them the disease.

LIFE AS A PEST

Black rats live in groups. They make nests for their young in trees or on the ground. Baby rats, or pups,

At the time of the bubonic plague pandemic in the 1300s, no one realized that bacteria within fleas that traveled on rats were to blame for the disease.

are born hairless and helpless. They become independent of their mothers by three to four weeks old. By three to five months, they are able to reproduce. Female black rats can have up to five litters a year. A litter contains between six and 12 pups.[14]

Black rats are considered pests. They destroy crops and human property. They can chew electrical wires in buildings, which increases the risk of fire. In addition, they hurt

FUN FACT
Black rats often live in high places. They may live in treetops or on the tops of buildings.

native wildlife. These rats eat many kinds of foods, including insects and other invertebrates, bird eggs and chicks, fruits, and seeds. They compete with other animals for food, and they prey upon other animals. As a result, black rats can cause other species to go extinct.

BLACK RAT
Rattus rattus

SIZE
1.2–1.3 feet (35–41 cm) from head to tail

WEIGHT
7 ounces (200 g)

RANGE
Native to India and surrounding region; introduced to all continents

HABITAT
Most concentrated in coastal areas, but found anywhere with enough plants to eat

DIET
Plant matter including grains, seeds, fruits; insects, other invertebrates, bird eggs and chicks

LIFE SPAN
1 year in the wild; up to 4 years in captivity

BLUE WHALE

Blue whales filter out food from the water using structures called baleen.

The enormous blue whale swims through the open ocean. It finds a large school of krill and opens its mouth. Swimming into the school, the whale scoops up a mouthful of the small sea creatures. The folds of its throat expand to let it take in a huge quantity of water loaded with krill. Then the whale closes its mouth. As many as 800 baleen plates line its mouth.[15] These plates are made from a material similar to that of fingernails. The whale's tongue pushes the mouthful of water and krill toward the baleen plates. The plates are close enough together that the water can squeeze through, but the krill cannot. Using this filtering process, the whale can then swallow the krill without the seawater. The blue whale will eat as much as four tons (3.6 metric tons) of krill in a single day.[16]

THE LARGEST ANIMAL

The blue whale is the largest animal on Earth. It is approximately as long as two large school buses, though it is relatively thin for its length. The whale is grayish blue with spots of lighter color. Microorganisms live on the whale's underside, giving this area a yellowish color. Its flippers are thin. The very short dorsal fin on its back sits close to the tail. A blue whale cannot breathe underwater. A hole at the top of the whale's head called a blowhole lets it breathe air at the surface.

FUN FACT

Blue whales typically swim at speeds of five miles per hour (8 kmh). They can swim at 20 miles per hour (32 kmh) in short bursts.[18]

Blue whales have a variety of vocalizations. They can make deep groans, moans, and pulses. They may use these sounds to help them navigate the dark oceans. Scientists think blue whales can sense objects by the length of time it takes the sound waves they emit to bounce off the objects and return to the whale. The whales also use sounds to communicate with one another. One blue whale may be able to hear another from as far as 1,000 miles (1,600 km) away.[17]

A blue whale rises to the surface to breathe.

LIFE IN THE DEPTHS

Blue whales are challenging to study because they live in the world's vast oceans. But scientists know a little about them. The whales usually live alone or in pairs. Blue whales are already about 23 feet (7 m) long when they are born.[19] The calves nurse for roughly eight months. They can have their own offspring at five years of age. Adult blue whales do not have any natural predators. But orcas and sharks may attack small calves.

Blue whales are an endangered species. Scientists estimate that there are at most 25,000 individuals in the world.[20] In the 1900s, people heavily hunted the whales for

blubber and oil. Today, hunting blue whales is no longer allowed. But they can be hurt or killed in collisions with ships. Blue whale numbers are rising slowly. People are working to protect these incredible creatures.

BLUE WHALE
Balaenoptera musculus

SIZE
82 feet (25 m) long on average for males; 90 feet (27 m) long on average for females

WEIGHT
210 tons (190 metric tons) on average

RANGE
All oceans except the Arctic Ocean

HABITAT
Open ocean

DIET
Mainly krill, occasionally small fish

LIFE SPAN
80–90 years in the wild

BOTTLENOSE DOLPHIN

Bottlenose dolphins are known for their playfulness and intelligence.

A dozen young bottlenose dolphins swim in the ocean a few miles from land. They speed along the water's surface, leaping into the air and diving back down again. One dolphin grabs a strip of kelp in its mouth and swims off. It releases the kelp, letting it float back to its flipper. The kelp hooks onto its flipper, and the dolphin swims to the surface to take a breath. Back underwater, the kelp slips from its flipper. The dolphin turns and swims under the kelp, letting the plant catch on its tail. Like other bottlenose dolphins, this individual enjoys playing with underwater plants.

The pod of dolphins slows down. One dolphin briefly rubs another with its nose. The group gathers together. They will rest for a while until they are ready to hunt.

APPEARANCE AND HUNTING

Bottlenose dolphins usually have gray bodies with white bellies. Their sleek, curved bodies are tapered at both the nose and tail. This shape reduces water resistance, allowing the animals to swim fast. Adult dolphins have little to no hair, which helps water move smoothly over their bodies. A tall dorsal fin rises from the dolphin's back. It helps the dolphin stay upright in the water. The dolphin breathes through a blowhole on the top of its head. It needs air every one to two minutes.

These marine mammals live in gulfs, bays, coastal areas, and the open ocean. Dolphins eat fish and invertebrates. Where they live determines what types of food they eat. Dolphins are very smart. They have many methods for hunting their prey. A group of dolphins may herd a school of fish into a tight group. Then individual dolphins take turns swimming through the school, grabbing fish to eat. Their teeth help them hold the prey. Others hunt alone. Some hold marine sponges in their mouths. They sweep the seafloor with the sponges to stir up prey.

FUN FACT

Bottlenose dolphins are excellent jumpers. They can leap as high as 16 feet (5 m) out of the water.[21]

A dolphin snatches a salmon off the coast of Scotland.

SOCIAL INTERACTIONS AND THREATS

Dolphins are social animals that often live in groups. Common groups include females with calves, young males and females, or entirely male groups. Dolphins communicate with one another using whistles. They can use physical behaviors such as rubbing to bond. Throughout their lives, dolphins exhibit playful behaviors. They play with a variety of items, including seaweed, rocks, and feathers. Dolphins also show aggression. They may bite, slap with their tails, or ram with their noses. If a dolphin is injured, other dolphins will try to help it. They may hold it at the water's surface so it can breathe.

A female dolphin gives birth to one calf at a time. The calf nurses for up to 20 months. Female calves become able to reproduce between five and ten years old. Males become able to reproduce between eight and 13 years of age.

Bottlenose dolphins have few predators. These include large sharks. Pollution, including toxins dumped into the ocean, harms dolphins. They can also get tangled in fishing gear. But bottlenose dolphins are not currently at risk of extinction. Many people enjoy watching dolphins leap into the air and swim alongside boats.

Many large aquariums keep bottlenose dolphins in captivity.

BOTTLENOSE DOLPHIN
Tursiops truncatus

SIZE
8–12.5 feet (2.4–3.8 m) long for males; 7.5–12 feet (2.3–3.7 m) long for females

WEIGHT
880 pounds (400 kg) on average

RANGE
Oceans around the world, except near the poles

HABITAT
Tropical, subtropical, and warm, temperate marine waters

DIET
Fish, invertebrates

LIFE SPAN
45 years on average in the wild; shorter in captivity

BROWN-THROATED THREE-TOED SLOTH

The three long claws on each limb give the three-toed sloth its name.

The brown-throated three-toed sloth slowly makes its way down the tree in the rain forest. It reaches for branches to grasp with its long claws. Finally, it arrives on the ground. It keeps its grasp on the tree while it digs a shallow hole with its tail. The sloth defecates and urinates in this hole, then it begins to slowly climb back up the tree again. It will need to repeat this process in about a week. Each time it is on the ground, the sloth is vulnerable to predators. It cannot move quickly. Animals such as jaguars may find and eat it.

APPEARANCE AND RELATIONSHIPS

The brown-throated three-toed sloth lives most of its life in the trees. It has long front limbs and shorter back legs. All four limbs end in three toes. Long, curved claws grow from the toes. The sloth has a small head, and its ears are not visible. The sloth's fur is grayish brown. A black stripe extends from either eye toward the outer edges of the face. Males have a patch of fur between the shoulders. This fur is orange with a brown stripe running through it.

Green algae are able to grow in the grooves of the sloth's

Sloths covered in algae take on a green color.

BROWN-THROATED THREE-TOED SLOTH

shaggy, coarse fur. The algae give the fur a green tint, which helps provide camouflage in the trees. The sloth may also get some nutrients from the algae when it grooms itself. The algae enable a symbiotic relationship between the sloth and a species of moth that feeds on the algae. The moths mate in the sloth's fur. When the sloth defecates, the moths lay their eggs in the sloth's feces. The moths

FUN FACT

Brown-throated three-toed sloths typically spend 14 to 16 hours per day sleeping and resting.[22]

also help add the element nitrogen into the sloth's fur. Nitrogen helps algae grow.

LIFE IN THE TREES

Brown-throated three-toed sloths eat mostly leaves. They get most of the moisture they need from these leaves. Their diet isn't very nutrient rich. As a result, they need to conserve their energy. They do this by moving slowly. The need to conserve energy also means that they cannot regulate their body temperature well.

Sloths are solitary. They can use their claws to defend their territories. The long claws can inflict deep wounds. Female sloths may give birth in the trees or on the ground. A female has one baby at a time. The offspring nurses for four months. It becomes independent as soon as two months later. At that point, the young takes over part of its mother's territory.

BROWN-THROATED THREE-TOED SLOTH
Bradypus variegatus

SIZE
2 feet (60 cm) long on average

WEIGHT
7.7–11.4 pounds (3.5–5.2 kg)

RANGE
Southern Central America, South America

HABITAT
Tropical forests; occasionally other forest types, lowlands, swamps

DIET
Leaves, flowers, fruits from trees of the genus *Cecropia*

LIFE SPAN
30–40 years in the wild

CAPYBARA

Capybaras are closely related to guinea pigs. They are similar in appearance but vastly different in size.

A female capybara has just given birth to four young. The young have fur, and they begin standing shortly after birth. Soon they gather with other young in the capybara group. They run and wrestle with each other. The group of ten includes males and females. Each adult helps raise the young. The young seek out any of the females to nurse. Males and females both watch out for danger.

A week after birth, the young are already eating grass in the marsh alongside the adults. Suddenly, one of the adults lets out a bark. It has spotted a jaguar. The capybaras quickly enter the water and submerge. Only their eyes and nostrils stay above the surface. Once the jaguar leaves, they emerge from hiding. The young are safe. They will continue to grow. In adulthood, they will be the world's largest rodents.

APPEARANCE AND DIET

Capybaras can weigh more than 100 pounds (45 kg)—as much as a Great Dane. But they are shorter and more compact. Their short, bristle-like fur is brown, and they do not have tails. They live in areas with water in South America. Grasses and aquatic plants make up much of their diets. Their bodies are adapted to their semiaquatic lifestyle. Webbed feet help them swim. A capybara's eyes, ears, and nostrils are on the top of its head. This lets the animal see, hear, and smell while the rest of its body is underwater.

As with all rodents, a capybara's teeth are always growing. Eating tough grasses wears them down so they don't become

A capybara dashes into a river to escape a jaguar.

FUN FACT

The capybara can hold its breath for a long time. It can stay completely underwater for up to five minutes.[23]

CAPYBARA

too long. Grasses are hard to digest. Capybaras will regurgitate food they have eaten earlier and chew it again. This helps them get as much nutrition from a given amount of food as possible. This practice is called rumination. But unlike other species that ruminate, such as sheep, capybaras have only one stomach chamber.

SOCIAL STRUCTURE

Capybaras are typically social animals. A group usually includes a dominant male, females, and other males. Young capybaras stay with a group until they reach a year old. A male has a gland on top of his snout that produces a scent. He rubs this gland on trees to mark his territory. Besides using scent, capybaras also communicate with sound. They use barks, whistles, and chuckling sounds.

Jaguars are the primary threat to adult capybaras. Young capybaras have more predators, including anacondas and caimans. Humans also hunt wild capybaras for meat and use their skins to make leather. Some people even raise capybaras on ranches for meat.

CAPYBARA
Hydrochoerus hydrochaeris

SIZE
Up to 2 feet (0.6 m) tall at the shoulder; 3.6–4.3 feet (1.1–1.3 m) long

WEIGHT
77–146 pounds (35–66 kg)

RANGE
South America

HABITAT
Typically habitats with water, including flooded grasslands, marshes, lowland forests; occasionally dry forests, grasslands, scrub

DIET
Mainly grasses, aquatic plants; occasionally bark, fruits

LIFE SPAN
Up to 10 years in the wild; up to 12 years in captivity

CAT

Domesticated cats can be found in homes around the world.

The small, brown tabby cat crouches behind a tractor tire in the barn. On the other side of the tire a mouse scurries along the floor. The cat slowly and silently creeps forward. It peers around the tire. The mouse is eating a few bits of grain on the floor. It does not see or hear the cat. The cat shifts on its haunches, then launches forward, pouncing on the mouse with its claws extended so the rodent can't escape. The cat picks up the mouse with its sharp teeth and stalks off to enjoy its meal.

DOMESTICATION AND APPEARANCE

The cat is a domesticated species. It has lost some of its wild nature, such as increased fear and aggression, to live alongside humans. A wildcat species lived in Egypt and the surrounding region as far back as 8,000 years ago. Crops attracted rodents. Wildcats began living near humans to hunt the rodents. The wildcats controlled the rodent population, and this was helpful to humans. The cats that were less fearful and aggressive toward humans were less likely to be killed by humans. The tame cats survived and passed on their tame genes to their offspring. Slowly the wildcats became domesticated. People began keeping cats for rodent control on farms and ships. Their use on ships contributed to their spread around the globe.

Today cats weigh nine to 12 pounds (4.1–5.4 kg) on average. Some are a bit larger, and others are a bit smaller. Their sharp claws are retractable. This helps keep their claws from catching on things all the time. Keen eyesight, excellent hearing, and a powerful sense of smell help them hunt.

Cats come in a variety of colors and coat patterns. Some have patches of color along with patches of white. Others have a striped pattern called tabby or patches of black, orange, and white called calico.

Cats are stealthy hunters, hiding and remaining quiet before they strike.

CAT

People have created various breeds of cats. They bred cats with similar traits together to create breeds that look unique from other cats. There is less variation between cat breeds than dog breeds. While dogs were bred to perform a wide variety of jobs, from gently retrieving fowl to pulling sleds, cats were historically kept only for the purpose of rodent control. But in modern history, people have been breeding cats for other traits. Cats may have long hair or short hair. Some are even hairless. Some have flat faces, while others have relatively long noses.

The Sphynx cat is a hairless breed.

LIFE WITH HUMANS

Cats are still used for rodent control around the world. In addition, many cats are companions to humans. They live inside the home. The companionship these cats provide is beneficial to

FUN FACT

It's a myth that cats always land on their feet. They can get hurt falling from high places.

people. Cats can lie on a human's lap, purr in response to petting, and perform amusing acrobatics. These things help reduce people's stress levels and improve their moods. Caring for cats can give people a sense of purpose. Cats need good food, water, and veterinary care. Indoor cats need clean litter boxes. Scratching posts keep cats from destroying furniture, and towers give cats safe places to climb. Playing with a cat gives it exercise, keeping it healthy and happy.

Domestic cats have caused some problems. Some have escaped captivity. They live as feral cats near human settlements. They can breed and overpopulate areas. This stresses the wildlife in the area. Both feral cats and captive cats that are allowed to roam outdoors hunt birds, small mammals, and reptiles. Cats are estimated to kill more than one billion birds annually.[24] They have led to the extinction of several species. They stress the populations of many kinds of birds. Responsible cat ownership is important to protect wildlife.

CAT
Felis catus

SIZE
2.5 feet (76 cm) from head to tail

WEIGHT
9–12 pounds (4.1–5.4 kg)

RANGE
All continents except Antarctica

HABITAT
Near human communities

DIET
In human care, mainly prepared foods that primarily contain meat; feral cats eat birds, fish, rodents, insects

LIFE SPAN
14 years on average in captivity

DOG

Dogs can be trained for a wide variety of jobs.

A woman who is visually impaired walks along a city sidewalk with her Labrador retriever. She holds a stiff handle attached to the dog's harness. The dog walks slightly ahead of her. Construction cones lie in the path ahead. The dog walks around the cones, making sure to leave enough room so that his handler doesn't walk into them. The pair arrives at an intersection, and the Lab stops. The woman listens for cars. When it sounds clear, she tells her dog to keep going. However, an electric car is approaching the intersection. It is much quieter than a gasoline-powered car, so the handler does not hear it. But the dog can see it. It refuses to walk into the intersection. The car speeds by. The handler asks her dog to move forward again. This time, there are no cars. The dog walks across the street with its handler.

DOMESTICATION AND APPEARANCE

Dogs have the most diverse physical traits of any species.[25] They range dramatically in size, coat type, and body structure. This variety stems from selective breeding for certain traits and working abilities. But most dogs share a few things in common: excellent senses of smell and hearing.

Dogs are domesticated. Scientists are not sure exactly where and when dogs were first domesticated. It may have happened in Asia or Europe. Estimates of when range from 20,000 to 40,000 years ago. Some believe the dog is the very first domesticated species.

Dogs are typically classified as a subspecies of gray wolf. However, many researchers do not believe dogs came directly from gray wolves. Rather, gray wolves and domestic dogs share a common wolf ancestor. Scientists think that this wolf ancestor began living near humans. These animals would eat scraps tossed out by the humans. People would not kill the dogs that were less aggressive and fearful.

Eventually people began breeding dogs for certain traits to help with important tasks. Dogs were bred for hunting, herding, or guarding abilities. Some were bred to be bigger so they could pull heavy loads. Others meant for hunting badgers were bred to be smaller

FUN FACT

Contrary to what was once believed, dogs can see in color. But they see fewer colors than humans. Dogs can see shades of blue and yellow in addition to gray.

DOG

DOG VARIETY

CHIHUAHUA
5–8 inches (13–20 cm) at shoulder
Short or long, single or double coat; straight or wavy

MASTIFF
At least 30 inches (76 cm) at shoulder
Short, double coat

STANDARD POODLE
More than 15 inches (38 cm) at shoulder; typically 22–27 inches (56–69 cm)
Very long, curly, single coat

GREAT DANE
28–32 inches (71–81 cm) or taller at shoulder
Short, straight, single coat

DACHSHUND
5–9 inches (13–23 cm) at shoulder
Short, single coat; long, double coat; or wire coat

SAMOYED
19–23.5 inches (48–60 cm) at shoulder
Long, thick, double coat

to fit into badger holes. People have bred dogs with similar traits to make hundreds of different breeds.

BEHAVIOR AND LIFE WITH HUMANS

While young wild mammals often play, adults do not play very much. However, many dogs remain playful throughout their lives. They will play with other dogs and humans. Dogs communicate largely with body language. A dog's ears, lips, eyes, tail, fur, and overall posture can reveal its mood, such as calm, playful, or fearful. Vocalizations, including whining, barking, and growling, also help with communication.

Today, many people keep dogs as companions. Some dogs still do the work they were bred for hundreds of years ago. Others have jobs that were created more recently. Some dogs assist people with disabilities. Others sniff out bombs or drugs. Dogs may perform in front of audiences or in films. Some people enjoy competing in sports with their dogs. Competitions include agility, which is similar to running an obstacle course, and scent work, where dogs sniff out certain odors such as birch.

Dogs help reduce stress and keep their owners company. Dog owners generally get more exercise because they have to regularly exercise their pets. Many people enjoy the companionship of a dog. Because dogs have a wide variety of personalities and exercise needs, understanding exactly what type of dog will fit best in the household will lead to the happiest situation for both people and their dogs.

DOG
Canis lupus familiaris

SIZE
3.8–44 inches (9.7–111 cm) tall at shoulders

WEIGHT
2–230 pounds (1–104 kg)

RANGE
All continents except Antarctica

HABITAT
Near human communities

DIET
In human care, mainly prepared foods that primarily contain meat; feral dogs hunt wild animals and livestock, and eat roadkill, plant matter, scraps humans leave behind

LIFE SPAN
10–13 years on average in captivity

DROMEDARY

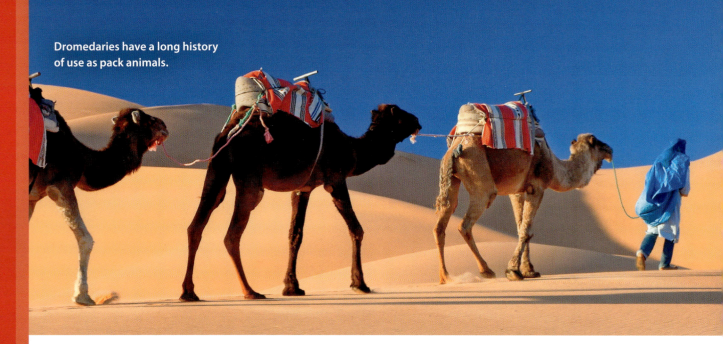

Dromedaries have a long history of use as pack animals.

A line of dromedary camels moves across the desert. Some carry riders. Others carry supplies. The desert is hot. The dromedaries have walked for 17 miles (27 km) already. But they haven't taken a drink. Camels can travel up to 100 miles (161 km) in a desert without drinking.[26] Camels do not typically sweat even in intense heat. This helps them retain water. They can get enough water to survive for several weeks at a time from the plants they eat. Then they will need a drink again. These camels will continue their dry, sandy journey for many more miles.

APPEARANCE AND ADAPTATIONS

Dromedaries are one of two camel species. Bactrian camels are wild, and they have two humps. Dromedaries are semidomesticated, meaning that they range freely

DROMEDARY

FUN FACT

Dromedaries can carry approximately 200-pound (90 kg) loads for 20 miles (30 km) per day.[27]

but are under the control of herders. Each has a single hump on its back. Camels are closely related to llamas and alpacas. Dromedaries have cream to brown fur and long, curved necks.

Many physical traits help dromedaries survive in their desert habitats. Their feet are wide, which keeps them from sinking in the sand. Long legs hold their bodies far away from the hot ground. They have long, thick eyelashes to keep sand out of their eyes. Their nostrils can close to shut out blowing sand.

A variety of adaptations allow dromedaries to cope with hot, dry, sandy conditions.

The hump is one of the most notable features of the dromedary. The hump can store up to 80 pounds (36 kg) of fat.[28] The camel's body converts the fat into energy and water when resources are scarce. Camels can also drink a lot of water when it is available. They can drink up to 30 gallons (114 L) of water in just a few minutes.[29]

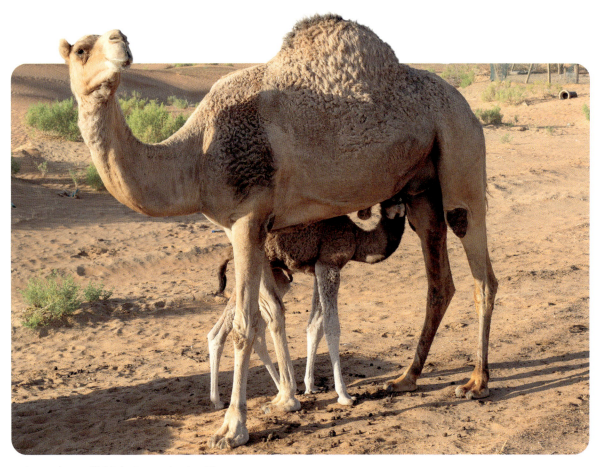

A dromedary calf drinks its mother's milk.

BEHAVIOR AND IMPORTANCE

Dromedaries were first domesticated approximately 4,000 years ago near what is now the United Arab Emirates. They were first ridden approximately 3,100 years ago. Today, they live in free-ranging herds. Dromedaries form groups of up to 20 members. These groups include a male, a few females, and their young.

These camels are rarely aggressive. They may push against one another or throw up the contents of their stomachs to spit. Females typically give birth to one calf at a time. Calves can walk within a few hours after birth. They nurse for one to two years.

People have relied on these camels for many things. They were an important means of transportation across the desert for a long time. Camels are nearly as fast as horses, but they can travel much farther without food and water. People use camels for more than transportation. Camel dung can be burned as fuel. People use dromedary hair to make cloth. They eat camel meat and drink the milk that camels produce.

DROMEDARY
Camelus dromedarius

SIZE
5.6–6.6 feet (1.7–2 m) tall at the shoulder

WEIGHT
660–1,300 pounds (300–600 kg)

RANGE
Africa, the Middle East, northern India; introduced to Australia

HABITAT
Arid deserts

DIET
Usually thorny plants, dry grasses, saltbushes; occasionally other desert plants

LIFE SPAN
40 years in the wild; 40–50 years in captivity

DUCK-BILLED PLATYPUS

The duck-billed platypus exhibits many traits that are rare or even unique among mammals.

It is mating season for duck-billed platypuses in Australia. Two males have found a female. The males start to wrestle along the edge of a stream. They jab at each other with the spurs on their hind legs. Each spur injects venom into the opponent. The venom causes pain. Eventually, one male has had enough. He crawls away from the fight. The winning male will get to mate with the female.

UNUSUAL MAMMALS

Duck-billed platypuses are unique mammals in many ways. In fact, early European scientists who heard of them thought the animals were made-up. Duck-billed platypuses closely resemble beavers. A platypus has brown fur and large, webbed feet. Its tail is wide like a beaver's, but it is covered in fur. Platypuses are monotremes. This means females lay eggs rather than give birth to live young. The platypus has a wide bill that looks similar to a duck's bill. While males and females are both born with spurs on their hind legs, only males keep the spurs into adulthood. The platypus is one of only a few venomous mammals.

At night the platypus looks for food on the bottoms of streams, rivers, and lakes. It uses its bill to quickly shovel through the material settled on the bottom. The animal's eyes, ears, and nostrils close while it hunts underwater. But its bill is sensitive to touch. The platypus can also sense small electrical currents that its prey generates when in motion. The platypus digs up worms, larvae, and insects, among other foods. It gathers this food in its cheeks and carries it to the surface, where it eats.

FUN FACT
The venom from a platypus's spurs cannot kill humans, but it does cause intense pain and swelling.

THE LIFE OF A PLATYPUS

Platypuses are solitary. They dig burrows on the banks of bodies of water. The entrances to their burrows are tight, which helps to squeeze water out of the platypuses' coats. When females are ready to lay their eggs, they dig a larger burrow. There are multiple rooms. The female usually lays two eggs. The eggs have leathery shells. The mother incubates her eggs for approximately ten days. She curls around them to keep them warm.

DUCK-BILLED PLATYPUS

If she has to leave the burrow, she covers the entrance with soil. After ten days, the babies hatch from the eggs. The babies are the size of beans, and they are hairless and helpless. The babies nurse for approximately four months before they leave to live on their own.

Platypuses are considered near threatened, meaning that in the future they could become at risk of going extinct in the wild. Primary threats include human activities, such as building dams and clearing trees, that affect their habitats. Platypuses are protected in Australia, which is their primary habitat. The country's 20-cent coin features the image of a platypus.

An Australian 20-cent coin

DUCK-BILLED PLATYPUS
Ornithorhynchus anatinus

SIZE
1.3–2 feet (39–60 cm) long

WEIGHT
1.8–5.5 pounds (0.8–2.5 kg)

RANGE
Australia, Tasmania

HABITAT
Lagoons, rivers, streams

DIET
Usually aquatic invertebrates; occasionally fish eggs, small fish

LIFE SPAN
Up to 12 years in the wild; 17 years on average in captivity

EASTERN GORILLA

Like other primates, eastern gorillas live in complex social structures.

The group of eastern gorillas sits in the dense forest near a volcano in Rwanda's Volcanoes National Park. Young gorillas just a couple of years old play and swing from branches in the trees. A female sits on the ground, nursing her baby while she eats leaves and stems from surrounding shrubs. A short distance from the group, the silverback, the male leader of the group, sits and eats. After munching on food for a while, it is time to move on. The silverback gets up and begins walking. The females and young follow. He will lead them to a good place to rest for the night.

EASTERN GORILLA

MASSIVE APES

FUN FACT
Gorillas build nests to sleep in each night. They make the nests with branches and leaves. These nests may be in the trees or on the ground.

Eastern gorillas are the largest primates. Primates are mammals with large brains and hands or feet that can grasp objects. Eastern gorillas weigh more than 400 pounds (180 kg). Females are smaller than males. These gorillas have long fur that can be bluish black to brownish gray. By the time a male is approximately 12 years old, the fur on his back has turned silver. He is called a silverback. Eastern gorillas have stocky bodies with long, muscular arms and short hind legs. Males have long canine teeth.

There are two subspecies of eastern gorilla. The eastern lowland gorilla is the largest. It lives in the lowland rain forests of the Democratic Republic of the Congo (DRC).

57

The mountain gorilla lives in the cloud forests among the volcanoes near the borders of the DRC, Rwanda, and Uganda. It has the longest hair of the gorillas, protecting it from cold temperatures.

FAMILY LIFE

Most eastern gorillas live in groups. A silverback leads the group. There are several females and other males, as well as the young. The silverback is the only male in the group

that breeds with the females. A female has one baby at a time. The baby nurses for three years but sometimes stays with its mother after that. The mother plays with her baby, grooms it, and teaches it what foods to eat. Males protect the group from rival males. They will beat their chests and charge any rivals. These gorillas rarely face threats from predators, as there are few large predators in their habitats.

Young females leave their birth groups to join a new group at approximately eight years old. Males will leave their birth groups at approximately 11 years old. They live alone until they find females with whom they can start their own groups.

Eastern gorillas are critically endangered. There are fewer than 3,000 living in the wild.[30] This is partially due to habitat destruction. People are clearing forests for agriculture. People also poach gorillas for their body parts. They sometimes take young gorillas from the wild for zoos or to keep as pets. Wars in the area have meant that it is not always possible to protect gorillas from poaching. Many organizations have formed to help protect these magnificent animals. They educate people about how to coexist with gorillas and how to protect their habitats.

EASTERN GORILLA
Gorilla beringei

SIZE
4.9–6.2 feet (1.5–1.9 m) long

WEIGHT
150–440 pounds (70–200 kg)

RANGE
Democratic Republic of the Congo, Rwanda, Uganda

HABITAT
Cloud forest of the Virunga volcanoes, lowland rain forests

DIET
Mainly bamboos, herbs, shrubs, vines; occasionally bark, flowers, fruits, fungi, invertebrates, wood, gorilla feces

LIFE SPAN
30–40 years on average in the wild; up to 50 years in captivity

ELK

Male elk use their broad antlers to compete for mates.

It is a late summer morning in Wyoming's Yellowstone National Park. A herd of hundreds of elk grazes. A bull, or male, elk lets out a piercing call called a bugle. He is letting females know he is ready to mate. A few females approach him. He rubs his massive antlers against bushes. He churns up dirt with his hooves. He urinates. He is spreading his scent, a message showing other bulls his strength. Other bulls in the herd are doing the same. One bull approaches the first. They walk side by side to determine who is larger. Then they face one another. They rush forward and lock antlers. The first bull is larger and stronger. Eventually, the smaller one gives up. The larger bull chases him away. He has secured the right to mate with the females drawn to his bugle.

APPEARANCE AND DIET

Elk are also called wapiti. The elk is the second-largest deer species, behind the moose. Its fur is shades of brown. It is darker in winter and lighter in summer. Elk grow dark manes of hair around their necks in winter. Their long

FUN FACT
Bull elk lose their antlers each year in March. New ones start to grow in May.

legs end in hooves. Each hoof is split into two digits. Bull elk have large antlers that can branch out as wide as the animal is tall. Females do not have antlers.

Elk are ruminants. They have adaptations to help them eat plants that are hard to digest. An elk's stomach has multiple chambers. When it eats, the food goes into the first chamber. It sits and softens. The elk later regurgitates the food and chews it further. This helps break down the plant so the elk can get more nutrients out of it. When the elk swallows the food again, it goes into the other chambers, which finish digesting it.

ELK LIFE

Elk herds can have hundreds of individuals during the summer. During the fall breeding season, a bull gathers a small group of females and defends his breeding rights with them. When the calves are born in late spring, mothers and calves form larger herds where they can protect their young from predators.

Wolves, bears, and cougars are the main predators of elk. They mostly prey on old,

sick, or young elk. However, elk have several defenses against predators. Males can use their antlers. Both males and females kick with their sharp hooves. Their long legs allow them to run fast for great distances, enabling them to escape predators.

Elk were once found in very large numbers in the Northern Hemisphere. Their numbers have dropped significantly as a result of hunting and habitat destruction. But there are still a lot of elk. They are not at risk of going extinct in the near future.

ELK
Cervus canadensis

SIZE
2.6–4.9 feet (0.8–1.5 m) tall at the shoulder

WEIGHT
150–1,100 pounds (70–500 kg)

RANGE
Native to the United States, Canada, Asia; introduced to Argentina, Australia, Chile, New Zealand

HABITAT
Open woodlands

DIET
Grasses, flowering plants, sedges, woody growths

LIFE SPAN
20 years or more in the wild; longer in captivity

EUROPEAN RABBIT

Burrows are important for European rabbits to keep themselves and their kittens safe.

A female European rabbit digs a burrow in the ground. She lines it with straw and her own fur. In this burrow, she gives birth to six babies, called kittens. The kittens have no fur. They are blind and helpless. The mother leaves shortly after giving birth. She covers the entrance of the burrow with dirt so predators will not find the babies. Then she spends her day eating grasses and other plants.

The mother returns to the burrow for only four or five minutes each day. At that time, she nurses the kittens. Then she leaves again. By the time the babies are four weeks old, they no longer need to nurse. They will be able to have their own offspring at as young as three months.

APPEARANCE AND DOMESTICATION

The European rabbit has mostly gray fur with bands of brown and black mixed in. It has long ears and lengthy, powerful hind legs that help it run with great speed to escape predators. The rabbit's tail is short.

The European rabbit is the ancestor of today's domestic rabbits. Domestic rabbits vary in size, fur length, and color. There are approximately 80 breeds of domestic rabbit.[31] Domestic rabbits are raised for their meat and fur, and they are also kept as pets.

A European rabbit's speed and agility are key means of defense against predators.

LIFE AS A RABBIT

European rabbits live in groups called colonies. There are up to ten rabbits in a colony. They live in a burrow system. The dominant male gets the most access to breeding with females.

Like other rabbits, European rabbits play an important role in the food chain. They are a source of food for many animals. Predators include canines, felines, and raptors. However, European rabbits have become invasive in many habitats where humans introduced them, including Australia. Their numbers have exploded in these areas, and they strain food resources for native species. Meanwhile, conservation experts have classified European rabbits as "near threatened" in their native range.

A few factors contribute to their invasiveness. These rabbits can eat a wide variety of plants. This means they usually do not starve when introduced to a new location. They also reproduce quickly. A female may give birth to 30 to 40 offspring in a year. The rabbits' native range of Europe has enough predators to keep their numbers in check. Some places where the rabbits have been introduced do not have enough predators. More rabbits are born than are eaten. European rabbits are now established in Australia, meaning that it is unlikely they will be eradicated.

FUN FACT

A few European rabbits were introduced to Australia in 1859. Seven years later, there were tens of thousands of these rabbits on the continent.[32]

EUROPEAN RABBIT
Oryctolagus cuniculus

SIZE
1.25–1.64 feet (38–50 cm) long

WEIGHT
3.3–5.5 pounds (1.5–2.5 kg)

RANGE
Native to southwestern Europe; introduced to most of the world except Asia and Antarctica

HABITAT
Dry areas at approximately sea level, including fields with brush cover, forests

DIET
Grasses, leaves, buds, bark, roots

LIFE SPAN
Less than 1 year on average in the wild; 9 years on average in captivity

FOUR-TOED HEDGEHOG

The four-toed hedgehog is a popular species among those who keep hedgehogs as pets.

It is night in Sudan. The four-toed hedgehog scurries along the desert ground. It is hunting for beetles and other insects to eat. Then a jackal comes into view. The hedgehog quickly curls into a tight ball. Stiff quills on its back fan out. The jackal sniffs at the hedgehog. The quills make it an unappealing meal, so the jackal trots off in search of other food. The hedgehog uncurls itself and continues its search for insects. It will travel several miles while it hunts.

APPEARANCE AND ADAPTATIONS

The four-toed hedgehog is also called the African pygmy hedgehog. The hedgehog is oval in shape, with a short tail and long, pointy nose. The top of its head, its back, and

FOUR-TOED HEDGEHOG

its sides are densely covered in quills—about 5,000 of them on an adult hedgehog.[33] The quills are typically brown or gray and have cream tips. The soft, short fur on the hedgehog's face and belly is white. A special muscle runs down the hedgehog's sides, across the throat, and along its rear. When it contracts the muscle, it forms a divot in the belly where its head and feet can fit. This lets the animal roll into a ball so that its quills poke out at all angles.

These hedgehogs are sensitive to temperature. They are most active when it is 75 to 85 degrees Fahrenheit (24–29°C). If it gets much hotter, the hedgehog will go underground and become dormant. It lowers the rate at which its body uses energy and lives off stored fat. It does not enter a deep sleep as animals in hibernation do. It occasionally wakes and goes to the surface.

FOUR-TOED HEDGEHOG

A four-toed hedgehog in captivity

PRICKLY PERSONALITIES

Most domesticated hedgehogs descend from the four-toed hedgehog. But they do not always make great pets. One reason is that they are solitary. They cannot be kept in an enclosure with another hedgehog, and they do not quickly warm up to human interaction. And because they are nocturnal, they cannot be kept in a bedroom, or their activity may keep people awake.

Hedgehogs have an unusual behavior called self-anointing. When a hedgehog comes across something giving off an

FUN FACT

Four-toed hedgehogs can tolerate eating toxins that would harm other animals. They sometimes feed on scorpions and poisonous snakes.

unfamiliar scent, it licks and chews the item. Eventually, the mouth generates a thick foam of saliva. Scientists think the foam contains this new scent. The hedgehog spreads this foam across the quills on its sides. Researchers speculate that this behavior attracts mates or defends against predators.

Baby hedgehogs are born blind and helpless. They have soft quills. After birth, the quills begin to harden. Babies nurse for four to six weeks. Then they leave to live on their own.

FOUR-TOED HEDGEHOG
Atelerix albiventris

SIZE
7–9 inches (18–23 cm) long

WEIGHT
11.8 ounces (335 g)

RANGE
Central Africa

HABITAT
Deserts

DIET
Mainly invertebrates including insects, spiders; occasionally plants, small vertebrates

LIFE SPAN
3–4 years in the wild; up to 4–6 years in captivity

HORSE

People frequently use horses in competitive events.

The horse and rider enter the cross-country course. It is the second of three phases of the eventing competition. They already completed the dressage phase, in which the rider subtly directed the horse through elegant movements in an arena. Now, in cross-country, the horse and rider face a different challenge. They take off at a gallop across the grassy course. They leap a solid log jump. The horse gallops toward the next jump. It clears the jump and lands in the pond of water on the other side. Splashing through the pond, it races toward the other side, where it climbs up the bank. After the final jump, the horse gallops as fast as it can toward the finish line. There is just one phase left, show jumping. The horse will clear tall fences in an arena, trying to not knock down any bars.

This three-phase competition is challenging. Horse and rider rely on trust. The eventing competition is based on a deep history of horses helping people. The first versions of these contests tested horses for their suitability for military use.

APPEARANCE AND DOMESTICATION

Horses have long heads and necks. A horse's hair is short except for a long mane down the back of the neck and a long tail. A horse's large eyes let it see almost entirely around its body. A horse has long, thin legs. Each leg ends in one oval-shaped hoof. Horses come in a wide variety of sizes and colors. Small horses are called ponies. They can be shorter than large dogs. Other horses may be approximately as tall at the shoulder as an adult human. Their colors include white and shades of brown and black. They may be a solid color or one of several patterns, including large patches of white and another color.

The history of horse domestication isn't well understood. Scientists generally believe it happened more than 5,000 years ago in Eurasia. Some scientists classify the domesticated horse as a subspecies of the wild horse, *Equus ferus*. Others consider it its own species, *Equus caballus*. Since domestication, horses have played an important role in human

HORSE

history. People used horses in wars and to pull chariots and carriages, carry riders, and plow fields. Today, there are no wild horses directly related to the domesticated horse. However, herds of feral horses, such as the mustangs in the United States, do live apart from humans. They descended from domesticated horses.

BEHAVIOR

Horses are prey animals, but they have ways to defend against predators. Foals can stand and run shortly after birth. They rely on their speed to escape threats. Feral horses form herds. Numbers help protect them from predators.

FUN FACT

Horses are measured in units called hands. One hand is equal to 4 inches (10 cm).[34] The term *pony* is used for horses shorter than 14.2 hands at the shoulder.[35]

A large herd of feral horses in Namibia

74

As in the wild, horses under human care need companions. Having other horses as companions is ideal. However, other species, such as goats, can partially satisfy that need.

Horses communicate with one another and humans in a variety of ways. They vocalize with various grunts, snorts, whinnies, and other sounds. They also use body language, including facial expressions that involve the ears, eyes, and nostrils. Horses fight by kicking and biting. They play by chasing, nipping, and shoving one another.

HORSE
Equus caballus

SIZE
3–5.6 feet (0.9–1.7 m) tall at shoulder

WEIGHT
500–2,000 pounds (230–900 kg)

RANGE
All continents except Antarctica

HABITAT
Most conditions under human care; when feral, typically cool grasslands, steppes, savannas, but occasionally semideserts, swamps, marshes, woodlands

DIET
Mainly grasses; occasionally grain when under human care

LIFE SPAN
25–30 years on average in captivity; shorter in the wild

INDIAN RHINOCEROS

Wallowing is important for keeping the Indian rhinoceros comfortable and safe in its hot habitat.

The sun is high in the sky. It is the hottest part of the day. The Indian rhinoceros walks through the grassland, arriving at its wallowing area. The shorter grasses here reveal depressions filled with muddy water. The rhino begins rolling in one of the muddy wallows. Mud covers its skin. The mud keeps the rhino cool in the heat. It also blocks harmful rays from the sun, deters biting insects, and keeps the rhino's skin from drying out. Once the day cools off, the rhino will leave to graze in the grassland.

INDIAN RHINOCEROS

APPEARANCE AND ADAPTATIONS

The Indian rhinoceros is also called the greater one-horned rhino. It has rough, brownish-gray skin. The hide is thick in sections, with skin folds that make it look like the rhino is wearing armor. A single horn grows from the top of the nose in both males and females.

The rhino's upper lip is able to grab bundles of tall grass to eat. Rhinos have excellent hearing and smell but poor vision.

FUN FACT

Indian rhinos are bulky, but they can reach impressive speeds. They have been observed charging at up to 30 miles per hour (50 kmh).[36]

Rhinos have a fearsome appearance, but they eat only plants.

77

They tend to charge toward sounds and smells to chase other animals off, so they are dangerous to approach.

SOLITARY GIANTS

Adult Indian rhinoceroses live alone. Rhinos do not always defend their territories, but sometimes rhinos do fight. They charge at one another and butt their horns together. They occasionally give one another deep wounds from their sharp lower teeth. Sometimes rhinos die in these fights.

A female typically gives birth to a single calf. The calf nurses for approximately a year. It stays with its mother for around two years after that. The mother will chase it away shortly before she gives birth to the next calf.

The Indian rhino is considered vulnerable. This means there is a large risk of extinction due to population losses. There are only approximately 2,200 individuals left in the wild.[37] One main reason the population is struggling is because of poaching. People hunt rhinos for their horns. People also sometimes kill rhinos to protect crops, which rhinos eat and trample. Habitat loss is another threat. Some rhino habitats have been converted to farmlands.

People are working to protect rhinos. Some places have troops dedicated to protecting rhinos from poachers. Organizations are working to ensure rhinos have enough natural habitat to survive. These groups also help educate local people about the importance of rhinos. They teach farmers which crops they can plant that rhinos are unlikely to eat.

INDIAN RHINOCEROS
Rhinoceros unicornis

SIZE
6 feet (1.8 m) at the shoulder

WEIGHT
2.2 tons (2 metric tons)

RANGE
Bangladesh, India, Nepal, Pakistan

HABITAT
Mainly plains, occasionally swamps, forests

DIET
Grasses, leaves, branches, fruits, aquatic plants, crops

LIFE SPAN
40 years on average in the wild; 47 years on average in captivity

LITTLE BROWN BAT

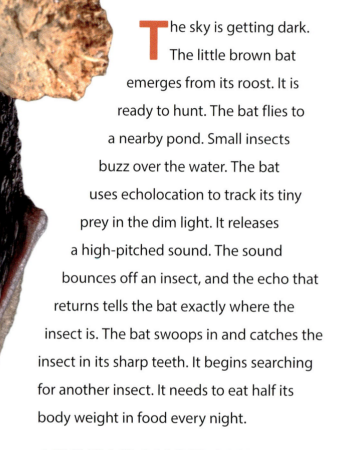

The little brown bat is one of more than 1,400 bat species on Earth.

The sky is getting dark. The little brown bat emerges from its roost. It is ready to hunt. The bat flies to a nearby pond. Small insects buzz over the water. The bat uses echolocation to track its tiny prey in the dim light. It releases a high-pitched sound. The sound bounces off an insect, and the echo that returns tells the bat exactly where the insect is. The bat swoops in and catches the insect in its sharp teeth. It begins searching for another insect. It needs to eat half its body weight in food every night.

APPEARANCE AND ADAPTATIONS

The little brown bat is medium-sized for a bat. It has glossy brown fur. The wings and ears are mostly hairless and dark brown. The bat's finger bones are long, and a membrane

spreads between them to form its wings. Its ears are relatively small, and it has large hind feet.

Little brown bats can flap their wings approximately 15 times per second.[38] They primarily get around by flying. However, they can crawl along the ground and also flap their wings to move along the water. These bats typically roost during the day. They find a dark place and hang upside down using their long toes and claws on their hind feet.

During the winter, little brown bats enter a form of hibernation called torpor. In torpor, their body functions slow down so the bats

FUN FACT

Bats can emit approximately 200 calls per second when using echolocation to find prey.[39]

use less energy. They roost with other bats in abandoned mines or caves that stay above freezing and have high humidity. They rely on their stores of fat to survive the winter.

BEHAVIOR AND THREATS

Little brown bats hunt on their own, but they do not usually defend hunting territories from other bats. One bat can eat between 300 and 3,000 insects per night.[40] This helps keep crop pest populations under control.

The little brown bat is considered endangered. Natural predators include weasels, raccoons, snakes, and domestic cats. These animals hunt roosting bats. Having large numbers of the bats concentrated in one spot can make hunting them relatively easy. Outside the roost, hawks and owls will catch bats in flight.

White-nose syndrome is causing bat populations to drop. This syndrome is caused by white fungus that grows on the bats' noses and wings. It irritates the

Little brown bats fly with their mouths open while using echolocation.

bats, causing them to wake during torpor. When they wake, their bodies use energy more quickly. They use up their fat stores before they are ready to emerge from torpor, so they starve to death.

LITTLE BROWN BAT
Myotis lucifugus

SIZE
Wingspan 9–11 inches (22–27 cm)

WEIGHT
0.2–0.5 ounces (5–14 g)

RANGE
Mainly North America

HABITAT
Mostly forested habitats near water, occasionally dry climates

DIET
Mainly insects that fly near water or sit on the water's surface

LIFE SPAN
6–7 years on average in the wild

NINE-BANDED ARMADILLO

The name *armadillo* is Spanish for "little armored one."

The nine-banded armadillo scurries along the forest floor. Its eyesight is poor, but it uses its excellent sense of smell to find food. The armadillo grunts as it sniffs the ground. It catches a scent and starts digging in the soft soil. Soon it uncovers beetle larvae. It collects the larvae with its long, sticky tongue, then swallows them. Once it finishes them off, the armadillo wanders away, following its nose to the next meal.

APPEARANCE AND ADAPTATIONS

Nine-banded armadillos have bony plates that cover their bodies. The plates are covered with leathery scales. There is one plate protecting the hips and one plate protecting the shoulders. Between those two plates are approximately eight to 11

NINE-BANDED ARMADILLO

bony bands. The bands form a joint, allowing the armadillo to bend. The tail and top of the head are also covered with a bony plate and scales, but the ears are not. These plates help protect armadillos from predators. The nine-banded armadillo cannot roll up into a ball like some other armadillo species.

Nine-banded armadillos sometimes stand upright as they sniff the air to locate food.

The nine-banded armadillo's underside is covered in hair rather than plates. Its front feet have four toes, and its back feet have five toes. The armadillo digs with the help of its long claws. Small peg-like teeth help it grind down food that is too big to swallow.

FUN FACT

The nine-banded armadillo can walk across the bottoms of streams or rivers. It can hold its breath for as long as six minutes.[41]

85

BEHAVIOR AND RANGE

Nine-banded armadillos dig burrows to rest in. Females give birth to young in their burrows too. They always give birth to four identical offspring. Baby armadillos look much like small adults, except that their plates are soft. It takes a few weeks for the plates to harden. The

babies nurse for up to three months and remain with their mothers a few more months before going off on their own. When they reach adulthood, males are bigger than females.

Many animals eat armadillos. Some of their predators include wolves, coyotes, black bears, and bobcats. If an armadillo feels threatened, it will leap into the air or run to its burrow or another shelter. Other burrows are used to collect food. These shallow burrows attract insects, which take shelter in them. The armadillo can visit these burrows and eat the insects that have gathered. Once an armadillo has abandoned a burrow, other animals may use it. Skunks, rabbits, and mink are among the animals that use armadillo burrows.

At one point, Texas was as far north as armadillos lived. But they have been gradually moving north. They are now frequently seen in Missouri and occasionally even farther north. They are not tolerant of extreme cold, so they are unlikely to become common in the northernmost states.

NINE-BANDED ARMADILLO
Dasypus novemcinctus

SIZE
2–2.6 feet (0.6–0.8 m) long from nose to tail

WEIGHT
8–17 pounds (4–8 kg)

RANGE
Southeastern United States, Mexico, Central America, northern South America

HABITAT
Mainly forest and scrub and brush habitats in tropical and temperate areas; occasionally grasslands and savannas near woody areas; adapts well to urban areas, gardens, pastures

DIET
Mostly insects, sometimes small reptiles or plant matter

LIFE SPAN
7–20 years or more in the wild; 23 years or more in captivity

RED KANGAROO

A young joey can often be seen hanging out of a mother kangaroo's pouch.

A female red kangaroo has just given birth to a joey. The joey is the size of a jelly bean. It has developed jaw muscles, a tongue, nostrils, and forelegs. But the rest of its body, including the eyes, have not developed. They are embryonic. The joey climbs up the mother's fur and into her belly pouch. In the pouch, the joey finds a nipple and latches on. It stays attached to the nipple for approximately two months. Then it begins venturing out from the pouch. By this time it has grown fur and

RED KANGAROO

developed. It quickly returns to the pouch if there is danger. At eight months, the joey no longer uses the pouch, but it continues to nurse until it is a year old.

APPEARANCE AND HABITAT

Red kangaroos are the largest marsupials.[42] Male red kangaroos typically have reddish-brown fur, helping camouflage them against Australia's red soil. Females usually have bluish-gray fur.

FUN FACT

Kangaroos can hop at speeds of more than 35 miles per hour (56 kmh). A single leap can cover 25 feet (8 m) and reach six feet (1.8 m) in height.[43]

Both males and females have white stripes from the corners of their mouths to their large ears. Their forelegs are short. Their paws can be used to grasp things. The kangaroo's lengthy, powerful hind legs let the animal hop around. A long, thick tail helps balance the body's forward-leaning position when the kangaroo hops, keeping its body from falling forward. A kangaroo also uses its tail when resting. It can sit back and balance on its back legs and tail.

Much of the red kangaroo's habitat is dry. Water is not always available. Kangaroos can get most of the water they need from the plants they eat. However, they do need to drink water occasionally. Kangaroos have a few ways to handle the heat of their habitats. As they hop, they will sweat. Once they stop to rest, they stop sweating. They begin panting and spreading saliva on their bodies, particularly their arms. Evaporation of the sweat or saliva helps cool them. In addition, during the hottest part of the day, kangaroos will rest in the shade of trees. They do most of their foraging in the early morning and late afternoon.

BEHAVIOR AND IMPORTANCE

Red kangaroos live in groups called mobs. There are approximately ten individuals in a mob, including several females, their offspring, and at least one male. Kangaroos warn each other of danger by hitting the ground with their hind feet. Males will fight with one another over the right to breed with females. Using their tails for balance, they hit each other with their forepaws. This type of fighting is called boxing. When fighting with one another or defending themselves from predators, kangaroos can also bite. They kick with their powerful back feet and claws too.

Red kangaroos have healthy population numbers. Their primary threat is human hunting. Humans hunt kangaroos for their meat and skins. The Australian government regulates this hunting to ensure kangaroo populations remain stable.

RED KANGAROO
Macropus rufus

SIZE
Up to 4.6 feet (1.4 m) in body length for males; up to 3.6 feet (1.1 m) in body length for females

WEIGHT
Up to 200 pounds (90 kg)

RANGE
Central Australia

HABITAT
Dry plains with scattered trees

DIET
Mainly grasses and flowering plants

LIFE SPAN
9–13 years in the wild; 20 years or more in captivity

RING-TAILED LEMUR

Ring-tailed lemurs typically have 13 black and 13 white stripes along their tails.

A male ring-tailed lemur sits on the ground. He rubs his wrists along his long, black-and-white striped tail. This action spreads an odor from the wrist's scent glands along the tail. Then the lemur walks on all fours toward another male, tail sticking straight up. As he approaches the male, he flicks his tail toward the other lemur. This action fans the odor toward that lemur. The rival backs off. Now the male can try to attract a nearby female.

APPEARANCE AND HABITAT

Ring-tailed lemurs are primates. They have gray to brown fur on their bodies with pale undersides and white facial fur. They have black noses and black rings around their eyes. Stripes of black and white encircle their tails. The tail is longer than the lemur's body. Both front and rear feet have four fingers and a thumb. This helps lemurs grip branches as they climb trees. Their tails cannot grasp branches like the tails of some other primates.

Ring-tailed lemurs, like all lemurs, live only on the island of Madagascar. Although they make their homes in trees, they spend most of their time on the ground looking for food. They most commonly eat the pod-like fruits from the tamarind tree. However, they are opportunistic and will eat many types of plants and small animals.

BEHAVIOR

Ring-tailed lemurs live in groups called troops. There are 15 to 20 males and females in a troop. Males change troops every two to five years. Females stay with the same troop their whole

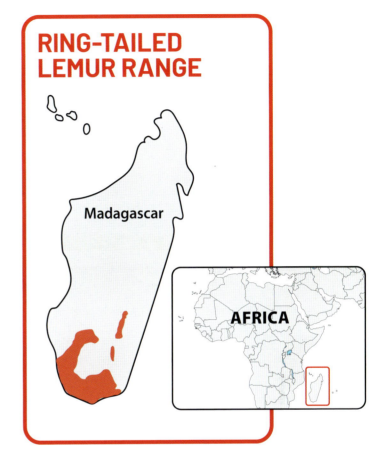

lives. Females are dominant over males. They get first access to food and can select the males they'd prefer to mate with. When a troop is on the move, members hold their tails high in the air. This helps keep everyone together. When a troop isn't foraging for food, its members may sunbathe. The lemurs sleep close together to stay warm at night.

RING-TAILED LEMUR

Lemurs sit together on a rock and groom each other.

FUN FACT

Ring-tailed lemurs are seed dispersers. They eat fruits, then leave the seeds behind in their feces.

The lemurs vocalize a lot. Communication is important when living in a group. They have at least 28 different sounds that they use to communicate.[44] They also use body language and facial expressions. Lemurs with close bonds groom each other. A lemur will use its lower teeth to comb through another lemur's fur.

A female lemur usually has one offspring per year. The offspring clings to the mother's chest until two weeks of age. Then the young rides on her back. It nurses until it is five months old. Sometimes other females in the troop will help take care of young that are not their own.

This species of lemur is endangered. Its numbers have been declining for many years. One of its biggest threats is habitat loss for agriculture. Some people hunt the lemurs, and others take lemurs from the wild and keep them as pets. Governments have protected parts of the lemurs' habitat from hunting and habitat loss. Organizations are working to help defend these animals.

RING-TAILED LEMUR
Lemur catta

SIZE
1.5 feet (46 cm) in body length

WEIGHT
5–7.5 pounds (2.3–3.4 kg)

RANGE
Southern Madagascar

HABITAT
Canopy forests, brush and scrub forests, mixed forests

DIET
Fruits, flowers, leaves, stems, insects, spiders, small vertebrates

LIFE SPAN
16–19 years in the wild; up to 27 years in captivity

TIGER

A fully grown tiger is among the most fearsome predators in the animal kingdom.

A herd of deer grazes in a forest in India. Nearby, a tiger watches them, hidden in the tall grasses and leaves. Its stripes help it blend in with the vegetation. A couple of young deer break away from the herd. They head to a small pond to drink water. The tiger slowly creeps after them from a distance. It places each foot slowly, so the deer don't hear it follow. They pause and glance around for danger. The tiger freezes. Not even its tail twitches.

The deer keep walking. They reach the pond and begin to drink. The tiger continues to stalk toward them. If it runs in their direction now, they will notice and outrun it. It needs to get closer without them noticing. Finally, once the tiger is close enough, it leaps forward. The deer dart away from the pond and try to run. But one doesn't get up to speed quickly enough. The tiger grabs the slow deer with its claws and bites the back of its neck. The tiger has caught its next meal.

APPEARANCE AND SUBSPECIES

Tigers are the largest species of cat.[45] The biggest males can weigh more than 600 pounds (272 kg). The tiger's orange fur is broken up by vertical black stripes. Its underside is lighter in color or white. Its forelegs are stocky and muscular. This helps the tiger when it grabs and holds prey with its sharp claws. The claws are retractable. They can be pulled back toward the toes so that they do not wear down as the cat walks. Sharp teeth and a powerful jaw help the tiger kill and eat prey.

There are six living subspecies of tiger. The largest is the Siberian or Amur tiger. It is the lightest in color because its habitat in Russia and China is snowy. The smallest is the Sumatran tiger. It has the darkest fur to help it blend in with the jungles of the island of Sumatra in Indonesia. Bengal tigers of India, Nepal, and Pakistan have the largest population. The other three subspecies are the Indochinese tiger of Southeast Asia, the Malayan tiger of the Malay Peninsula, and the South China tiger, which may be extinct in the wild.

FUN FACT

Tigers can leap huge distances. They have been observed covering 33 feet (10 m) in one bound.[46]

TIGER

A Siberian tiger hunts a bird at a protected park in eastern China.

BEHAVIOR AND THREATS

Tigers are solitary cats. They most commonly hunt at night, but they occasionally hunt during the day. Each tiger has its own territory. A tiger marks its territory with urine, feces, and claw marks. Tigers will typically fight off invaders, but some will share territory with another tiger.

A female tiger gives birth to an average of two to three cubs at a time. Cubs are helpless. They nurse until approximately three months old. The mother begins teaching them to hunt at around five months old. They become independent at about two years old and leave to establish their own territories.

Tigers are endangered. They live in just a fraction of their original ranges. Habitat loss from human activities, poaching for skins and local medicines, and conflicts with human settlements are the main threats to tigers. Some governments have made it illegal to kill tigers. Countries around the world have banned the sale of tiger parts. Organizations work to protect tiger habitats. Many people seek to help these animals, which are often used to symbolize strength and courage, so they can survive for generations to come.

TIGER
Panthera tigris

SIZE
6.5–12 feet (2–3.7 m) long from head to tail

WEIGHT
220–660 pounds (100–299 kg)

RANGE
Russia, northeastern China, Southeast Asia, parts of India and the Himalayan region

HABITAT
Temperate, tropical, or evergreen forests, mangrove swamps, grasslands

DIET
Mainly ungulates, including many deer species, water buffalo, wild pigs; also bears; occasionally livestock, Malayan tapirs, Indian elephants, young Indian rhinoceroses, large birds, leopards, fish

LIFE SPAN
8–10 years in the wild; 16–18 years on average in captivity

ESSENTIAL FACTS

MAMMAL FEATURES

- All mammals have hair at some point in their lives. They all have three middle ear bones, and all females produce milk from mammary glands to feed their young.

- Most mammals have a single lower jawbone, as well as good senses of sight, smell, hearing, and touch.

- Mammals are divided into three basic groups based on how their young develop. These groups are placental mammals, marsupials, and monotremes.

NOTABLE SPECIES

- The African bush elephant (*Loxodonta africana*) is the largest land animal on Earth.

- The blue whale (*Balaenoptera musculus*) is the largest animal on Earth.

- The dog (*Canis lupus familiaris*) may have been the first domesticated animal. It has played an important role in human civilizations for millennia.

- The duck-billed platypus (*Ornithorhynchus anatinus*) is an unusual mammal that has a duck-like bill, lays eggs, and is venomous.

MAMMALS' ROLES ON EARTH

Mammals live in nearly every habitat on Earth. They have been an important source of food for both humans and other animals. Predators such as tigers (*Panthera tigris*) help keep the populations of other animals in check. Mammals have also helped local economies by attracting tourists. People travel to spot the brown-throated three-toed sloth (*Bradypus variegatus*) in Central America or the African bush elephant (*Loxodonta africana*) in Namibia. Mammals such as cats (*Felis catus*) and dogs (*Canis lupus familiaris*) are beloved pets and companions to people around the world.

MAMMALS AND CONSERVATION

Some mammals, such as the cat (*Felis catus*), have driven other animals to extinction. European rabbits (*Oryctolagus cuniculus*) have become invasive in many areas, competing with native species for food. The Indian rhinoceros (*Rhinoceros unicornis*) faces the risk of extinction because of poaching and habitat destruction. Many people work to protect endangered mammals from extinction by protecting habitat and banning or limiting hunting.

MAMMALS AROUND THE WORLD

GLOSSARY

adaptation
A change in traits within a population that allows an individual or species to be more successful in its environment.

climate
The average weather in a region over a period of years.

domesticated
Adapted to live among or be of use to people.

ecosystem
A community of interacting organisms and their environment.

embryonic
Having to do with an early stage of development in which parts of an animal such as organs are still developing.

endangered
At risk of becoming extinct.

extinction
The state of having completely died out.

feral
Wild or untamed.

gland
A tissue or organ that secretes a substance.

incubate
To keep eggs warm until they are ready to hatch.

invertebrate
An animal without a spinal column.

ivory
The hard, white material that makes up the tusks of certain mammals.

microorganism
A living thing too small to be seen with the naked eye.

poaching
The illegal taking of wild animals.

protein
An amino acid chain present in organic material, such as skin, hair, or blood.

subspecies
A group within a species that is able to breed with other members of that species but has genetic or other differences from those other members.

symbiotic
Mutually beneficial between two or more organisms not of the same species.

temperate
Having mild temperatures.

uterus
The organ in a female mammal in which the young develop before birth.

ADDITIONAL RESOURCES

SELECTED BIBLIOGRAPHY

"Animal Diversity Web." *University of Michigan Museum of Zoology*, 2020, animaldiversity.org. Accessed 15 Dec. 2020.

"Hall of Mammals." *Berkeley University of California*, n.d., ucmp.berkeley.edu. Accessed 15 Dec. 2020.

"The IUCN Red List of Threatened Species." *IUCN Red List*, n.d., iucnredlist.org. Accessed 15 Dec. 2020.

FURTHER READINGS

Carwardine, Mark. *Handbook of Whales, Dolphins, and Porpoises of the World*. Princeton, 2020.

Edwards, Sue Bradford. *The Evolution of Mammals*. Abdo, 2019.

Howell, Catherine Herbert. *National Geographic Pocket Guide to the Mammals of North America*. National Geographic, 2016.

ONLINE RESOURCES

To learn more about mammals, please visit **abdobooklinks.com** or scan this QR code. These links are routinely monitored and updated to provide the most current information available.

MORE INFORMATION

For more information on this subject, contact or visit the following organizations:

American Museum of Natural History
200 Central Park W.
New York, NY 10024
212-769-5100
amnh.org/research/vertebrate-zoology/mammalogy

The American Museum of Natural History's Department of Mammalogy has the third-largest collection of mammal specimens in the world.

The Marine Mammal Center
2000 Bunker Rd.
Fort Cronkhite
Sausalito, CA 94965
415-289-7325
marinemammalcenter.org

The Marine Mammal Center helps rescue and rehabilitate sick and injured marine mammals in addition to supporting scientific research and education. It works with volunteers in California and Hawaii.

SOURCE NOTES

1. Matthew Wund and Phil Myers. "Mammalia." *Animal Diversity Web*, 2005, animaldiversity.org. Accessed 22 Feb. 2021.

2. "ASM Mammal Diversity Database." *American Society of Mammalogists*, n.d., mammaldiversity.org. Accessed 22 Feb. 2021.

3. "Browse by Family." *AmphibiaWeb*, 2021, amphibiaweb.org. Accessed 22 Feb. 2021.

4. "Entomology Facts and Figures." *Royal Entomological Society*, 2021, royensoc.co.uk. Accessed 22 Feb. 2021.

5. "Sea Otters in Alaska." *PBS*, n.d., pbs.org. Accessed 22 Feb. 2021.

6. Wund and Myers, "Mammalia."

7. Sydney Weil. "Cheetahs: The World's Fastest Land Animal." *African Wildlife Foundation*, 21 Sept. 2013, awf.org. Accessed 22 Feb. 2021.

8. Adam Millward. "Life in the Slow Lane: Three Amazing Sloth Records." *Guinness World Records*, 19 Oct. 2018, guinnessworldrecords.com. Accessed 22 Feb. 2021.

9. "African Elephant." *National Geographic*, n.d., nationalgeographic.com. Accessed 22 Feb. 2021.

10. Meghan Howard. "Loxodonta Africana." *Animal Diversity Web*, 2017, animaldiversity.org. Accessed 22 Feb. 2021.

11. Jeheskel Shoshani. "Elephant." *Britannica*, 2020, britannica.com. Accessed 22 Feb. 2021.

12. Rebecca Anderson. "Castor Canadensis." *Animal Diversity Web*, 2002, animaldiversityweb.org. Accessed 22 Feb. 2021.

13. Guy Musser. "Beaver." *Britannica*, 2020, britannica.com. Accessed 22 Feb. 2021.

14. Heather Gillespie. "Rattus Rattus." *Animal Diversity Web*, 2004, animaldiversity.org. Accessed 22 Feb. 2021.

15. "Whalebone." *Britannica*, 2018, britannica.com. Accessed 22 Feb. 2021.

16. "Blue Whale." *National Geographic*, n.d., nationalgeographic.com. Accessed 22 Feb. 2021.

17. "Blue Whale."

18. "Blue Whale." *NOAA Fisheries*, n.d., fisheries.noaa.gov. Accessed 22 Feb. 2021.

19. Tanya Dewey and David L. Fox. "Balaenoptera Musculus." *Animal Diversity Web*, 2002, animaldiversity.org. Accessed 22 Feb. 2021.

20. "'Astonishing' Rise in Blue Whale Numbers." *BBC Newsround*, 20 Feb. 2020, bbc.co.uk. Accessed 22 Feb. 2021.

21. "Common Bottlenose Dolphin." *National Geographic*, n.d., nationalgeographic.com. Accessed 22 Feb. 2021.

22. Hee-Jin Jung. "Bradypus Variegatus." *Animal Diversity Web*, 2011, animaldiversity.org. Accessed 22 Feb. 2021.

23. Kathryn Frens. "Hydrochoerus Hydrochaeris." *Animal Diversity Web*, 2009, animaldiversity.org. Accessed 22 Feb. 2021.

24. S. R. Loss et al. "The Impact of Free-Ranging Domestic Cats on Wildlife of the United States." *Nature Communications*, 4(1396), 2013. Accessed 22 Feb. 2021.

25. "Domestic Dog." *National Geographic*, n.d., nationalgeographic.com. Accessed 22 Feb. 2021.

26. "Arabian Camel." *National Geographic*, n.d., nationalgeographic.com. Accessed 22 Feb. 2021.

27. "Camel." *San Diego Zoo*, 2021, animals.sandiegozoo.org. Accessed 22 Feb. 2021.

28. "Arabian Camel."

29. "Arabian Camel."

30. "Eastern Gorilla." *IUCN Red List*, 2018, iucnredlist.org. Accessed 22 Feb. 2021.

31. Flavia Schepmans. "Introduced Species Summary Project: European Rabbit." *Columbia University*, 17 Feb. 2003, columbia.edu. Accessed 22 Feb. 2021.

32. "European Rabbit." *Agriculture Victoria*, 7 Feb. 2021, agriculture.vic.gov.au. Accessed 22 Feb. 2021.

33. "Hedgehog." *San Diego Zoo*, 2021, animals.sandiegozoo.org. Accessed 22 Feb. 2021.

34. Emily Donoho. "Why Are Horses Measured in Hands?" *Horse & Hound*, 26 Dec. 2017, horseandhound.co.uk. Accessed 22 Feb. 2021.

35. Alois Wilhelm Podhajsky. "Horse." *Britannica*, 2020, britannica.com. Accessed 22 Feb. 2021.

36. "Indian Rhinoceros." *National Geographic*, n.d., nationalgeographic.com. Accessed 22 Feb. 2021.

37. S. Ellis and B. Talukdar. "Greater One-Horned Rhino." *IUCN Red List*, 2018, iucnredlist.org. Accessed 22 Feb. 2021.

38. "Little Brown Bat." *Adirondack Ecological Center*, 1988, esf.edu. Accessed 22 Feb. 2021.

39. Aaron Havens. "Myotis Lucifugus." *Animal Diversity Web*, 2006, animaldiversity.org. Accessed 22 Feb. 2021.

40. "Little Brown Bat." *Virtual Nature Trail at Penn State New Kensington*, 22 July 2014, dept.psu.edu. Accessed 22 Feb. 2021.

41. "Nine-Banded Armadillo." *National Wildlife Federation*, n.d., nwf.org. Accessed 22 Feb. 2021.

42. Tanya Dewey and Minerva Yue. "Macropus Rufus." *Animal Diversity Web*, 2001, animaldiversity.org. Accessed 22 Feb. 2021.

43. "Red Kangaroo." *National Geographic*, n.d., nationalgeographic.com. Accessed 22 Feb. 2021.

44. "Ring-Tailed Lemur." *Oregon Zoo*, n.d., oregonzoo.org. Accessed 22 Feb. 2021.

45. "Tiger." *Britannica*, 2020, britannica.com. Accessed 22 Feb. 2021.

46. Kevin Dacres. "Panthera Tigris." *Animal Diversity Web*, 2007, animaldiversity.org. Accessed 22 Feb. 2021.

INDEX

adaptations
   for defense, 68–69, 84–85
   for eating, 62
   for flight, 80–81
   for heat, 13–14, 49–50, 90
   for hunting, 41, 97
   for water, 18, 37
Africa, 5, 12–15, 57, 93
algae, 33–34
antlers, 60–63
armadillos, 84–87
Asia, 45, 73, 97
Australia, 52, 55, 66, 89

baleen, 24–25
bats, 7, 80–83
bears, 8, 62, 87
beavers, 16–19, 53
birds, 7, 23, 43, 82
blowholes, 25, 29
body temperature, 35
burrows, 4, 9, 53–54, 64, 66, 86–87

camels, 48–51
capybaras, 36–39
cats, 40–43, 82, 96–99
classification of mammals, 5–6
communication, 7, 10, 15, 18, 25, 30, 39, 46, 75, 95
crops, 10, 22, 41, 79, 82

deer, 60–63, 96–97
deserts, 4, 48–49, 51, 68
disease, 10, 11, 21–22
dogs, 6, 11, 42, 44–47, 73
dolphins, 28–31
domestication, 4, 40–41, 45, 51, 65, 70, 73

ears, 7, 13–14, 18, 21, 37, 46, 53, 65, 80–81
echolocation, 80–81
eggs, 9, 23, 34, 53–54
elephants, 6, 12–15
elk, 60–63
endangered species, 26, 59, 82, 95, 99
Europe, 22, 45, 64–66
eventing, 72–73

fighting, 9, 52, 60–61, 75, 78, 90, 98

gorillas, 11, 56–59
grooming, 19, 34, 59, 95

hair, 6
hedgehogs, 68–71
herds, 12–15, 51, 60, 62, 74
hibernation, 81
horns, 77–79
horses, 8, 51, 72–75
humans, 4
hunting by humans, 4, 11, 19, 26–27, 39, 63, 79, 91, 95

India, 21, 76–79, 96, 97
invasive species, 66
invertebrates, 23, 29

jaguars, 33, 36–37, 39
jumping, 4, 29, 72, 87, 89, 97

kangaroos, 8, 88–91
krill, 24–25

lemurs, 92–95

Madagascar, 93
marsupials, 7, 8, 89
microorganisms, 25
milk, 7, 9
monotremes, 7, 8–9, 53

pests, 10–11, 22–23, 82
pets, 42–43, 46–47, 59, 65, 70
placental mammals, 7–8
platypuses, 9, 52–55
play, 28, 30, 43, 46, 56, 59, 75
primates, 57, 92–93
protecting mammals, 59, 79, 95, 99

rabbits, 64–66, 87
rats, 11, 20–23
relationship to humans, 10–11
reptiles, 7, 43
rhinoceroses, 76–79
rodents, 16–17, 37, 40–41, 42
rumination, 39, 62

seeds, 23, 95
sharks, 26, 31
sloths, 7, 32–35
social structures, 9–10, 30, 39
solitary mammals, 35, 53, 70, 78, 98
South America, 37

territories, 10, 35, 39, 78, 82, 98–99
tigers, 11, 96–99

United States, 74, 87
urban areas, 21

venom, 52–53

whales, 6, 7, 11, 24–27
wolves, 11, 45, 62, 87

zoos, 59

ABOUT THE AUTHOR
Marie Pearson

Marie Pearson is an author and editor of books for young readers. Her favorite topics are about nature, especially animals. The coolest mammal she has seen in the wild was the Chinese white dolphin, which is also called the pink dolphin. She has shared her life with several dogs and cats and currently lives with her Australian shepherd and standard poodle, whom she enjoys training for a variety of dog sports.

ABOUT THE CONSULTANT
Dr. Hayley C. Lanier

Dr. Hayley C. Lanier is an assistant curator of mammals at the Sam Noble Museum of Natural History at the University of Oklahoma. Much of her research has focused on alpine mammals, such as pikas (small relatives of rabbits found in the mountains of western North America and Asia). She shares her life with her husband and her young son, who at the age of two is already quite fond of joining her and her students to "catch rats."